To my mum, that great recycler, and all her
great-grandchildren, the recyclers of the future - JJ

For Olivia - GP

First published in 2010 by Scholastic Children's Books
Euston House, 24 Eversholt Street
London NW1 1DB
a division of Scholastic Ltd
www.scholastic.co.uk
London ~ New York ~ Toronto ~ Sydney ~ Auckland
Mexico City ~ New Delhi ~ Hong Kong

Text copyright © 2010 Julia Jarman
Illustrations copyright © 2010 Garry Parsons

HB ISBN 978 1407 10975 6
PB ISBN 978 1407 10996 1

All rights reserved
Printed in Singapore

1 3 5 7 9 10 8 6 4 2

The moral rights of Julia Jarman and Garry Parsons have been asserted.

Papers used by Scholastic Children's Books are made from
wood grown in sustainable forests.

HEY!
WHAT'S THAT NASTY WHIFF?

SCHOLASTIC

Hyena was a cleaner,
       She kept things spick and span.
She picked up after others
       With a little brush and pan.

She hoovered the savannah,

She mopped the
grassy plains,

And though nobody thanked her,
She never once complained.

She recycled all
the rubbish,

She loved her
compost heap.

She never wasted water,

And she grew good things to eat.

But no one seemed to notice
    All the tireless work she did
To keep the grasslands spotless...

And so

one day

she hid.

Feeling sad and lonely,
    She had a little howl.
But someone overheard her...

Who?

A scruffy-headed fowl!

Vulture fluttered over.
"Don't **fret** yourself, my dear.
I know just how you're feeling –
I've cleaned up top for **years.**

"I finish up their dinners,
    I sweep up all their crumbs.
We two care for Planet Earth
    While they sit on their—"

"Tums," agreed Hyena.
"I hate to moan and gripe,
But they don't notice folk like us,
The plain but useful types."

Vulture said, "Let's go on strike,
Stop doing what we do.
They might appreciate us
When they start to smell the...

"Rubbish?"
said Hyena
(She liked to
be polite).

"I'd love to
put my feet up,
But would it
be all right?"

"It might teach them a lesson,"
Said Vulture. "Look, let's try.
Let's go to the seaside –

Quick!

Gone
away

Let's pack.

We'll fly!"

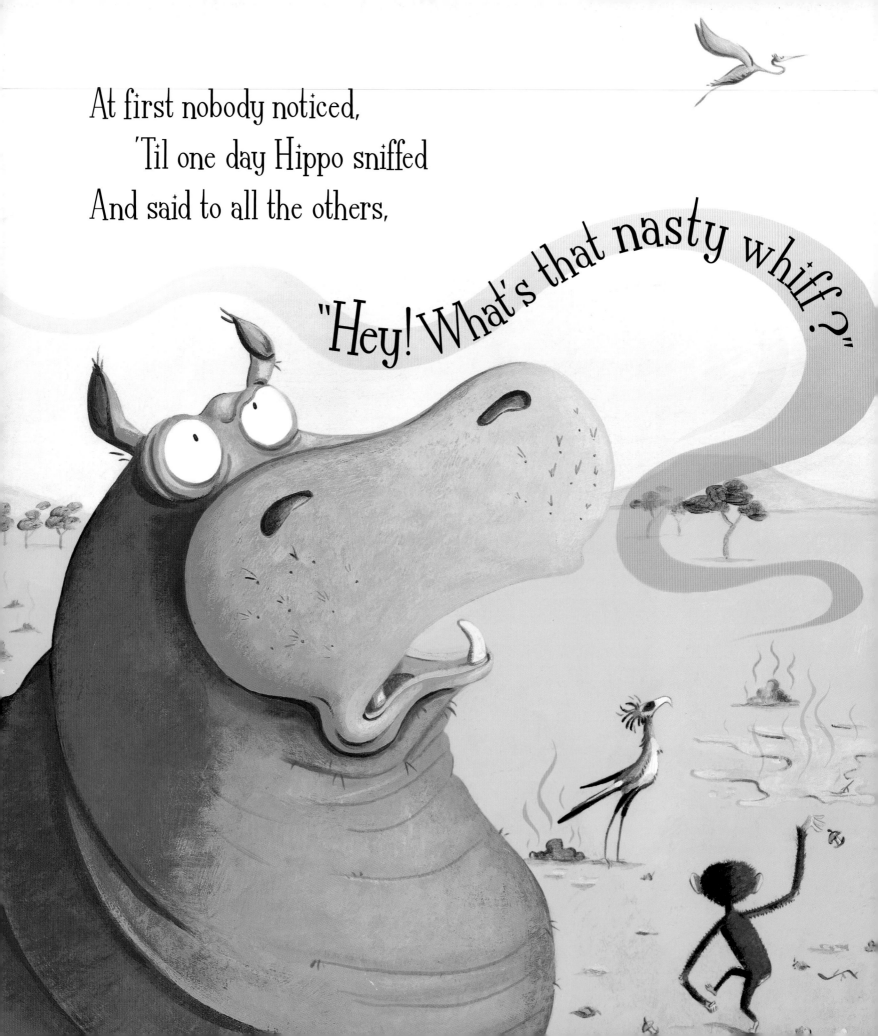

At first nobody noticed,
   'Til one day Hippo sniffed
And said to all the others,

"Hey! What's that nasty whiff?"

The smell grew really **stinky**,

And it wasn't very **long**

 Before the others noticed

A most **disgusting**...

PONG!

And as the pong grew **stronger**,
They wondered what to do.
The rubbish piled up higher,

And so

did all

the...

POO!

Meanwhile at the seaside,
On Sunnyside Marina,
Vulture put on suncream
And passed it to Hyena.

Then...

From way up high above them,
They heard a desperate shout:

"We're all knee-deep
in rubbish!
Please come and
help us out!"

Hyena cried, "YES! YES!
This is so exciting!"

But: "Steady on," said Vulture,
"Let's get this all in writing.

"I'll draw up a contract...

See? We're not going back
'Til you and all the others
Say **yes** to all of **that.**"

Flamingo flew off swiftly,

But Hyena was concerned:
  Would the others all agree?
And would the bird return?

Then just before the sunset,
    Not too far away…
They saw the other animals!
    Would **they** help save the day?

avannah! Save the Planet!

Hartebeest
Bushbuck Warthog Okapi Jackal Oribi
Leopard

We all promise truly to recycle and to clean,
And to help to save our planet Reed
By always being green! Lion
Signed: Croc Topi
Egret Baboon
Flamingo Ant
Parrot Puku Mouse